Scott and Steven play
First they get their space sled.
They pull it up the snowy hill.

Scott calls for their space dog, Spanky.
Spanky slides in the snow.
Then he steps onto the space sled.

Steven calls for their space cat, Spice.
Spice slips in the snow.
Then she steps onto the space sled.

Scott and Steven get on the space sled.
5, 4, 3, 2, 1 . . . blast off!
Scott steers the sled.

The space sled speeds down the hill.
It swings from side to side.
It swishes through the snow.

Scott and Steven see many sparkles.
The sparkles look like stars in space.
They are really snowflakes in the sky.

The space sled skids to a stop.
Scott and Steven smile.
Spice and Spanky jump off the sled.

The space ride is over.
Scott and Steven go back home.
The space sled is ready for another space ride!